The moral rights of the author and illustrator have been asserted

Published by Ladybird Books Ltd
27 Wrights Lane London W8 5TZ
A Penguin Company

2 4 6 8 10 9 7 5 3 1

First published MCMLXXXII © Jean and Gareth Adamson
This edition MMI

LADYBIRD and the device of a Ladybird are trademarks of Ladybird Books Ltd

Printed in Italy

Learn about time

Jean and Gareth Adamson

"Ding-dong, ding-dong, ding-dong, DING,"
said the big church clock.

"One, two, three, four, five, six,
SEVEN o'clock," said Topsy.
"Time to get up, Tim!"

seven o'clock

Topsy and Tim were up and
washed in five minutes...

five past seven

In another five minutes
they were dressed...

ten past seven

In another five minutes
they were downstairs,
eating breakfast...

quarter past seven

and in another five
minutes they had finished.

twenty past seven

eight o'clock

"What's all the rush?" asked Dad.

"Mummy's taking us to visit Granny and Grandpa," said Topsy.

"We'll catch the nine o'clock bus," said Tim.

"Steady on," said Dad, looking at the kitchen clock, "it's only eight o'clock. Time I was off to work."

eight fifty-five

Topsy and Tim got to the bus stop early.
They had a long wait.

"Do you think we've missed the bus?"
asked Tim gloomily. Mummy looked at her
watch. "It's only five minutes to nine,"
she said.

Five minutes later,
at exactly nine o'clock,
along came the bus.

nine o'clock

"All aboard," said the bus driver.

There was a big clock in the road where
Mummy and Topsy and Tim got off the bus.
The time was ten o'clock.

"That bus ride took a whole hour,"
said Mummy. Topsy and Tim didn't say
anything. They both felt a bit bus-sick.

Ten minutes later Tim was ringing
Granny's doorbell and Topsy was rattling
her letter-box.

"Whoever can it be?" laughed Granny.

"It's US!" shouted Topsy through the letter-box.

"My word," said Grandpa, looking at his pocket watch, "you are nice and early. It's only ten minutes past ten."

Topsy and Tim explored
Granny's house.
It was full of interesting
things. Best of all they
liked the grandfather clock.

"It is very old,"
Grandpa told them.

"As old as you, Grandpa?"
asked Tim.

"Even older," said Grandpa.

The grandfather clock had funny,
old-fashioned numbers.

"What time does it say?" asked Topsy.

"It's half past ten," Grandpa told them.

half past ten

Topsy and Tim found Granny and Mummy
in the kitchen drinking tea.

"Would you like some elevenses?"
asked Granny.

eleven o'clock

"What are elevenses?" asked Topsy.

"The drinks and biscuits you have at eleven o'clock," said Granny.

"We like elevenses!" said Topsy and Tim.

There was an old clock on Granny's dresser.
It said four o'clock.

"That clock is not right," said Tim.

"Poor old clock," said Granny. "It doesn't
go any longer. Would you like to play with it?"

"Yes please," said Topsy and Tim.

Topsy and Tim found a knob on the back of the old clock. It turned the hands. They made the clock tell lots of different times.

five o'clock

two thirty-five

twenty-five past three

five minutes to one

ten to seven

quarter to six

All of a sudden the clock started ringing
VERY LOUDLY. It gave Topsy and Tim
such a surprise that they dropped it
on the floor.

Tim picked the clock up.

"Listen," said Topsy. "It's started ticking."

"I think we've mended your old clock,
Granny," said Tim.

"What is the right time?" asked Granny. Grandpa's pocket watch said twelve o'clock. Mummy's wrist watch said twelve o'clock. The grandfather clock said twelve o'clock.

Topsy and Tim made the old alarm clock say twelve o'clock too.

At three o'clock it was time for Mummy to take Topsy and Tim home. The old clock was still ticking and telling the right time.

"Thank you for having us," said Topsy and Tim.

"Thank you for coming and mending our old clock," said Granny and Grandpa as they waved goodbye.

That night, in bed, Topsy and Tim counted
as the big church clock struck eight.

"Time to go to sleep, Tim," yawned Topsy.
But Tim was fast asleep already.